D0475231

Garfield County Libraries
Glenwood Springs Branch
815 Cooper Avenue
Glenwood Springs, CO 81601
(970) 945-5958 • Fax (970) 945-7723
www.GCPLD.org

# The LEATHER APRON Club

# About the
# Strange
# Capitalizations
# in
# THIS BOOK

*The Cambridge Encyclopedia of the English Language* discusses the growth of a standard mode of capitalization in English. John Hart, who lived in sixteenth-century England, was an English educator best known as a spelling reformer. According to the encyclopedia, "Hart recommended his readers to use a capital letter at the beginning of every sentence, proper name, and important common noun."

By the next century "the practice had extended to titles (*Sir, Lady*), forms of address (*Father, Mistris* [sic]), and personified nouns (*Nature*). Emphasized words and phrases would also attract a capital. By the beginning of the 18th century . . . this practice [was] extended still further . . . and it was not long before some writers began using a capital for any noun that they felt to be important."

When we meet Billy, he is neither well educated nor a grammarian, so his capitalizations are mostly for things that interest him, like Kites, Books, Cider, and Cake.

# The LEATHER APRON Club

## Benjamin Franklin, His Son Billy & America's First Circulating Library

Jane Yolen

ILLUSTRATED BY Wendell Minor

ini Charlesbridge

**Year of Our Lord**

# 1739

My name is William Franklin.
My family calls me Billy.
Pappy calls me Good Boy
when I help him in the Print Shop,
which is on the ground Floor
of our House in Philadelphia.
Mama shakes a finger at me and scolds.
She always scolds, whatever I do,
and her scolds are hot enough to blister the skin,
especially in the Morning when Pappy and I
eat our bread-and-milk Porridge in our twopenny Bowls.
She continues scolding the whole Day through.
Pappy says it's a Wonder her finger
doesn't fall off with all that scolding.

I am eight years old,
which is old enough to help Pappy.
He was an apprentice at my age,
working in his brother's Boston Print Shop.
Pappy is the famous Ben Franklin,
who has written the best-known Book
in all of Philadelphia,
printed on his own Press—
*Poor Richard's Almanack.*
It is full of sayings to make people wise,
though if you ask me, I think it is a little boring.
Poor Richard makes remarks like this:
*"An egg today is better than a hen tomorrow."*
Well, maybe that is not so boring.
I shall heed the advice and stop work today
rather than wait for tomorrow
to run off with cousin James to play.

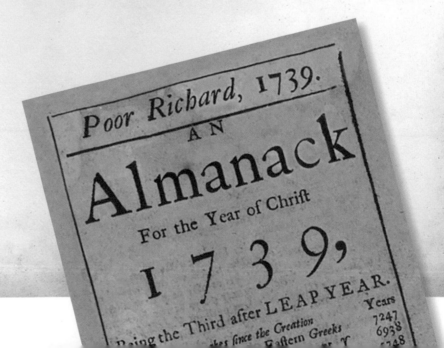

We have a Print Shop in our house.
I find James at work with Mama,
under her scolding gaze.
I signal him with a wink.
Before Mama can stop us,
we have torn off our Leather Aprons
and raced out the door.
Mama's voice follows me,
calling out, "Base-born brat!"
She is not my birth mama
and never fails to remind me of it.
Then I remember the *Almanack*:
*"Blame-all and praise-all are two blockheads."*
Whoever is blamed, whoever the blockhead,
I neither know nor care.
James and I are off.

The streets are full of People
of every color in the world.
James and I head toward the long Port,
clogged with great Ships.
We imitate Sailors with their rolling walks.
We fling Sticks in the air
and skip Stones on the water.
Poor Richard warns:
*"Little rogues easily become great ones."*
But James and I have a fine time.
Everything a boy can want is in Philadelphia:
Shops and Ships, Show horses and Sheep.
There are Creeks to wade, Rivers to swim,
the great Ocean to fish.
And most of all, there are long, green meadows
where we can fly Kites.
I think a Boy who cannot find pleasure
flying a Kite can never be happy!

The Shops open before Sunrise
and do not shut again till Sunset.
Many Shopkeepers
are Pappy's good Friends,
and they never fail to offer a treat.
After fishing and swimming,
and skipping Stones and flying Kites,
James and I stop for many
a sweet Cake and Cider.
As Poor Richard advises:
*"He that waits upon fortune,*
*is never sure of a dinner."*
When we get home, wet, messy, full of Cake,
Mama scolds, of course.
Even Pappy looks a Storm.
"Boys," he says, "you are like Lion Cubs."
He means we are all roar and no wit.
"I have engaged a Tamer."
I look at James,
but he looks at the floor.

"The Tamer's name," says Pappy,
"is Theophilus Grew,
and he is to be your tutor."
*Theophilus Grew!* He sounds like an ogre
from some halfpenny Chapbook.
I make a face, and James makes another.
Neither of us wants to be tutored.
That means staying indoors.
It means reading dull Books,
writing dull essays, and Ciphering.
It means memorizing great lists of Things
we will never use again,
like the names of England's Kings
and the dates of long-ago Battles.
"No!" I cry. "Not a Tutor!"
James's gray Face says the same.
But Pappy quotes to us from his own Book:
There are *"no gains without pains."*

The very next day we are carted off
to Master Grew's home.
We learn Mathematics and History,
Latin and Grammar.
Pappy reminds us that
*"God gives all things to industry."*
"I hope Master Grew gives us Cake and Cider
for all *our* industry," whispers James.
Master Grew does not seem the Cake type,
even less the Cider.
His house is full of Books, Paper, Inkstands, Pens.
Maps and Charts hang on every wall.
Everything seems too hot, too close,
as if Ideas make their own heat.
*This will not work*, I think,
and I remember Poor Richard:
*"If you'd have a servant
that you like, serve yourself."*
I look out the Window,
thinking how well it would serve us
if I could plot our escape.

Master Grew is both Tutor and Tamer, with willful gray Hair,
and eyes dark and sharp as a crow's.
He picks up a Book from a big pile
and begins to translate from the Greek.
*"Sing, Muse, sing of wily Odysseus,*
*his ship driven again*
*and again off course,*
*after he had plundered*
*the hallowed heights*
*of the great city of Troy."*
His voice is deep.

I begin to see Pictures in my Head:
Ships sailing a wine-dark Sea,
the gray-eyed Goddess Athena,
the shattered Towers of Troy.
I am bespelled, but about a hundred lines in,
James begins to snore.
For a moment Master Grew falters.
"Go on, go on," I urge. "Go on!"
I am enchanted, as if Circe, the witch in the story,
has changed me into someone else.

All through the next Week,
Master Grew reads to us.
James fidgets and naps, but I'm so enthralled
that when Master Grew stops,
I begin to read the Book by myself.
Pappy has one at home
in good common English.
I tell Pappy and Mama about the story.
Mama sniffs at Pappy, saying,
"He is the spit of you," as if that is a bad thing.
Pappy laughs. "When you are done, Billy,
I have a book about the battle in Troy."
I look around. "Here?" I ask.
"In the Leather Apron Club library," he says.
I can hardly breathe.
I have never been to the Leather Apron Club,
though I have heard of it.
Indeed, all Philadelphia has.
I think of the words of Poor Richard:
*"Diligence is the mother of good luck."*
And what good Luck it is that I have such a Father.

The very next evening,
Pappy and I go to the little House
that the Leather Apron Club rents.
When we walk in, I stand still for a moment.
So many Books line the walls.
Their Covers are all colors:
brown, black, blue, green, red, and tan.
They smell of Stories, at once musty and new.
I count at least one hundred Books.
I have never seen so many in one place.
"Pappy," I say, taking a deep breath,
"It is . . . it is . . ."
I cannot find the word.
"I know, Son. I know," he says. "It's magical."
Pappy and I sit in comfortable leather Chairs
and read till we are too excited to read anymore.
We drink Cider and discuss what we have learned.

The next evening and the next, I read at the Club,
my mind consumed with story,
where heroes likely and unlikely save the day.
Then one evening when the clock tolls eight,
the rest of the twelve Men of the Club arrive.
They are a glassworker, a scrivener, a clerk, and more,
all lovers of books like Pappy and me.
Pappy has warned me to keep quiet and listen,
for every meeting begins with the same Questions.

"Do you love Mankind in general regardless of religion or profession?"

In my Head I answer: *I think so.*

"Do you love and pursue Truth for its own sake?"

*I will try to.*

There are more Questions, all hard ones.

Poor Richard knows that

*"The noblest question in the world is,*

*what good may I do in it?"*

I consider carefully and reply in my mind,

thinking of something Pappy often says:

*Do more.*

The men debate Politics and History and Books.
They drink Cider, eat Cake, and debate more—
Mathematics and Geography and Finance.
Though the discussion is above me,
I feel as if I am in Heaven.
I am stuffed with more than Cake.
Full of learning,
I fall asleep and dream
of Odysseus arguing history
and politics with the Gods
as his men row through the wine-dark Sea.
I do not recall how Pappy and I get home.
But that is all right, for as Pappy says:
*"A word to the wise is enough."*
And surely I am wiser tonight
for having been at the Leather Apron Club.

Sad to say, as day follows day,
James does not seem to love Books.
I am remarkably fond of them.
They open up Worlds once closed to me,
worlds long gone, never been, or not yet.
James says that I am no longer amusing.
Perhaps James is not a good Friend after all.
Poor Richard says,
*"He that lies down with dogs,*
*shall rise up with fleas."*
I am sad to lose James's friendship,
but I have Books now, and a longing to learn.
I feel that it is time for me to "Do more."
More reading, more learning, more growing,
so one day I may become a real member
of the Leather Apron Club.

## *About* WILLIAM FRANKLIN, BOY AND MAN

We know only a little about Billy Franklin's early life. He was Benjamin Franklin's first child, born in 1730 or 1731. The date and his birth mother's identity have remained a mystery. His stepmother, Deborah Franklin, never really loved him. She used terrible words when talking about him, even when he was a small child. But Ben Franklin lavished money and love on the boy. Ben Franklin's second son, Frankie, died at age four of smallpox. Daughter Sally was born when Billy was a teenager. The Franklin house was always full of people.

Billy and his cousin James were adventurous and wild. Sent first to Master Grew to be tutored, Billy often accompanied Ben Franklin on his outings, including at the famous kite-flying experiment. By the time Billy was eight, the Leather Apron Club's library was established. We do not know for sure that he visited it.

In later years Bill became a captain in the Pennsylvania forces and clerk of the provincial assembly. He trained in London as a lawyer and then was the last royal governor of New Jersey. Billy—by then called William—was a Tory, remaining loyal to Britain despite his father's dedication to the Revolution.

In 1776 William was declared an enemy of the country and arrested for aiding the British. He remained under guard in Connecticut for two years. Eventually he was let go, and he helped form the Associated Loyalists, who launched guerilla attacks on Americans. In 1782 William sailed for England, where he lived on an English-government pension, perhaps because he'd been a spy.

William did not see his father again until 1785 in England when William's son, William Temple Franklin, accompanied his grandfather, Benjamin, to Paris as his secretary. Both Billy and Benjamin were saddened at the loss of their relationship, but it was never mended.

## *About* THE LEATHER APRON CLUB

The Leather Apron Club, also known as the Junto Club, began in 1727 when twelve friends began meeting weekly to discuss issues of morality, philosophy, and politics. They pooled their few books and put them in one place so all could enjoy them. A few years later, they took subscriptions to the growing library. With the money, they bought more books. Soon anyone could read at the Club, though only true subscribers could take a book home. The Club lasted for forty years.

Ben Franklin called the Leather Apron Club "the best school of philosophy, morality, and politics that ever existed in the province." By 1742 the Library Company of Philadelphia—as it was then known—had grown to more than three hundred volumes. In 1773 it ran out of space and moved to the second floor of the building where the Continental Congress would meet the following year. By 1789 they began constructing a building to house the collection. Today the Library Company on Locust Street in Philadelphia houses many of the books in the club's original collection—including Homer's *The Odyssey*.

## About BENJAMIN FRANKLIN AND SLAVERY

Though Benjamin Franklin contributed much to modern society, it is important to note that he shared the belief, common at the time, that Black people were inferior to white Europeans. He himself had two enslaved men, George and King, who lived in the family house. They worked both in the print room and the shop. Additionally, Franklin's newspaper, *The Pennsylvania Gazette*, often ran notices involving the sale or purchase of enslaved people.

Franklin's beliefs on the subject were challenged later in life and began to evolve. As a result, he eventually became president of an abolitionist group, the Society for Promoting the Abolition of Slavery and the Relief of Negroes Unlawfully Held in Bondage.

## About POOR RICHARD'S ALMANAC

Franklin's famous book, *Poor Richard's Almanack* was written and printed by Benjamin Franklin from 1733–1758. Today we write its name without the final "k." An almanac is a book published every year that contains facts about weather, astronomy, and other general information. Franklin did not invent the form, but he invented the author—the imaginary Richard Saunders. It was the most successful almanac of the century.

Many people quoted Poor Richard, who was both a wit and a sage. He commented on everything from the political to the practical, and about how to live a proper and full life. Probably the most quoted saying from the book is from the 1735 edition: "Early to bed and early to rise makes a man healthy, wealthy, and wise."

## A *Very* PARTIAL AND PARTICULAR BIBLIOGRAPHY

Fleming, Candace. *Ben Franklin's Almanac: Being a True Account of the Good Gentleman's Life*. New York: Atheneum, 2003.

Franklin, Benjamin. *The Autobiography of Benjamin Franklin with Related Documents*. Edited by Louis P. Masur. New York: Bedford St. Martin's Press, 2003.

Isaacson, Walter. *Benjamin Franklin: An American Life*. New York: Simon & Schuster, 2003.

Skemp, Sheila L. *William Franklin: Son of a Patriot, Servant of a King*. Oxford, England: Oxford University Press, 1990.

## A *Note* FROM THE AUTHOR

Wendell Minor and I were sitting next to each other at the White House listening to speakers at the National Book Festival when Walter Isaacson, the author of *Benjamin Franklin: An American Life*, got up to read. He mentioned the Leather Apron Club and that it was the first free lending library in the United States.

"That's a picture book," I whispered to Wendell.

He whispered back, "You write it, and I'll illustrate it!"

That was in 2004. Yes, it can take a long time for a picture book to be made.

*For two wonderful editors, Patricia Lee Gauch and Yolanda Scott, because every sheep needs a good shepherd—J. Y.*

*To all reluctant young readers who discover the magic of books!—W. M.*

Text copyright © 2021 by Jane Yolen
Illustrations copyright © 2021 by Wendell Minor
All rights reserved, including the right of reproduction in whole or in part in any form. Charlesbridge and colophon are registered trademarks of Charlesbridge Publishing, Inc.

At the time of publication, all URLs printed in this book were accurate and active. Charlesbridge, the author, and the illustrator are not responsible for the content or accessibility of any website.

Published by Charlesbridge
9 Galen Street
Watertown, MA 02472
(617) 926-0329
www.charlesbridge.com

Printed in China
(hc) 10 9 8 7 6 5 4 3 2 1

Illustrations done in watercolor on Strathmore 500 Bristol paper
Display type set in Allegheny by Scriptorium Fonts
Text type set in Mrs. Eaves by Emigre Graphics
Color separations and printing by 1010 Printing
    International Limited in Huizhou, Guangdong, China
Production supervision by Jennifer Most Delaney
Designed by Diane M. Earley

**Library of Congress Cataloging-in-Publication Data**
Names: Yolen, Jane, author. | Minor, Wendell, illustrator.
Title: The Leather Apron Club: Benjamin Franklin, his son Billy, and America's first circulating library / by Jane Yolen; illustrated by Wendell Minor.
Other titles: Benjamin Franklin, his son Billy, and America's first circulating library
Description: Watertown, MA: Charlesbridge Publishing, [2021] | Includes bibliographical references. | Audience: Ages 7-10. | Audience: Grades 2-3. | Summary: "Billy Franklin discovers a love of learning and books through the Leather Apron Club library, run by his father, the famous Benjamin Franklin."— Provided by publisher.
Identifiers: LCCN 2020017271 (print) | LCCN 2020017272 (ebook) | ISBN 9781580897198 (hardcover) | ISBN 9781607349358 (ebook)
Subjects: LCSH: Philadelphia (Pa.)—History—Colonial period, ca. 1600-1775—Juvenile literature | Franklin, William, 1731-1813—Childhood and youth—Juvenile literature. | Franklin, Benjamin, 1706-1790—Family—Juvenile literature. | Books and reading—Pennsylvania—Philadelphia—Juvenile literature. | Junto (Club: Philadelphia, Pa.)—Juvenile literature. | Library Company of Philadelphia—History—Juvenile literature. | Statesmen's children—United States—Biography.
Classification: LCC F158.4 .Y65 2021 (print) | LCC F158.4 (ebook) | DDC 973.3092/2—dc23
LC record available at https://lccn.loc.gov/2020017271
LC ebook record available at https://lccn.loc.gov/2020017272]